The Puppies of Blossom Meadow

The Puppies of Blossom Meadow

By Catherine Coe

Book 4:
Dandelion Dance

SCHOLASTIC

Published in the UK by Scholastic, 2022
1 London Bridge, London, SE1 9BA
Scholastic Ireland, 89E Lagan Road, Dublin Industrial Estate,
Glasnevin, Dublin, D11 HP5F

Text © Catherine Coe, 2022
Cover illustration © Andrew Farley represented by Meiklejohn, 2022
Illustrations by Jestenia Southerland © Scholastic, 2022

The right of Catherine Coe to be identified as the author
of this work has been asserted by her under the
Copyright, Designs and Patents Act 1988.

ISBN 978 1407 19869 9

Printed by CPI Group (UK) Ltd, Croydon, CR0 4YY

Paper made from wood grown in sustainable forests
and other controlled sources.

1 3 5 7 9 10 8 6 4 2

www.scholastic.co.uk

Blossom Meado
Primrose Pond
Badger Burrows
Poppy Place
Dai
H

The Great Hedge

Buttercup Bridge

Bluebell Grove

Sunflower Square

Lupin Lane

Blossom Brook

Violet Green

Honeysuckle Hill

To Phoebe and Amber xxx

Chapter 1

Busy Blossom Meadow

"Girls, are you in there?" Kayla's dad called from the garden.

"Oh no," said Kayla. "Quick!" Inside the storeroom, she thrust out the purple dog collar so that her two best friends, Erin and Amber, could grab it. The collar shimmered, the silver Blossom name tag spun, and tingles zipped up their arms as the magic began to take hold. White sparkles circled around them, like they were in the middle of a mini tornado.

Amber squealed and shut her eyes. This bit was always the weirdest. It felt incredible to be wrapped up in warm, glittering magic — but it also made her panic a little, especially when her feet lifted off the floor.

"Are you OK in there?" came Kayla's dad's voice, closer now.

"He's going to come in!" yelped Erin as the white sparkles became a thick spinning cloud around them. "What if he sees us disappear?"

But they couldn't see the storeroom any more, and Kayla hoped that meant her dad wouldn't be able to see *them* either. He would get a huge shock if he did! At least no time would pass at home while they were away, so hopefully her dad wouldn't miss them.

The next second, Amber felt her feet touch the ground. She opened her eyes slowly and saw the sparkles fading away. They were no longer in the storeroom of Doggy Delight, the dog kennels where Kayla's dad worked, and where they'd been helping out. Instead, they were standing among long grasses and green bushes dotted with white flowers. A rich, sweet smell filled the friends' nostrils. This was Honeysuckle Hill in Blossom Meadow. And their sense of smell was much better than normal, because they were no longer girls, but puppies!

"What's going on?" Erin barked, jumping up on her hind legs and looking around. Erin was a golden Labrador, with a shiny almost-white coat and a little wagging tail. Amber was a sleek black terrier, with a white tummy and perky black ears. And Kayla was a chestnut-brown cockapoo, with super-curly fur and a panting pink tongue.

The friends looked on in surprise. They'd never seen Blossom Meadow so busy before — it was alive with creatures moving this way and that, both on the ground and in the sky. Bright butterflies swooped across the sky among buzzing bees and gliding birds. Animals ran across the meadow as far as the eye could see — foxes and badgers and mice and rabbits, squirrels and frogs and moles and deer.

Kayla waved at a passing hedgehog. "Excuse me..." she began to say.

The spiky hedgehog turned his head as he plodded through the grass. "I'm sorry, I can't stop. Too much to do!" And he kept on shuffling along. Kayla wondered whether to run beside him — he wasn't walking very fast — but decided that would be too rude when he was clearly busy.

Meanwhile, Erin was trying to get the attention of one of the birds flying above. She leapt up and down, waving her paws. "Hello! Hello! Please come and talk to us!"

"No time!" twittered a blackbird. "Got to rush!"

"What's happening here?" wondered Amber, bouncing from paw to paw. "I hope there isn't something wrong."

The puppies had helped out with problems in the meadow before. Last time they'd been here, they'd helped reunite the meadowers when the water sprites had played too many pranks on everyone. Before that, they'd helped the trolls and the fairies. Erin, Kayla and Amber couldn't believe that they were friends with magical creatures as well as animals, birds and insects. It was a dream come true! They loved being in Blossom Meadow more than anywhere else, which is why they'd been so relieved to finally have an excuse to get to the storeroom in Doggy Delight at the end of the day. Kayla's dad had asked them to return the grooming accessories to the shelf before they left.

But we only just made it, thought Kayla, as she scooped up the purple Blossom collar from the ground and on to her neck for safe-keeping. The collar was usually kept in the storeroom at Doggy Delight – they'd found it on top of a cupboard the very first day they'd helped out at the kennels. It was how they got to Blossom Meadow, and how they got home too, so they needed to take care of it! All they had to do was hold it at the same time, and it magically transported them there and back.

"Let's go and find George," Amber suggested, pointing a black paw in the direction of Badger Burrows. "If he's at home, he'll be able to tell us."

The three puppies scampered away across the beautiful honeysuckles, leaving their sweet scent behind as they ran on to Daisy Heath. They tried not to stomp on any of the tiny white daisies as they gambolled

over the grass – but it wasn't too difficult as there weren't many daisies growing there today.

Is that what's wrong? Erin wondered. *Have the flowers started disappearing?*

A large area of dry brown soil spread out

in front of them and they raced across to the hole that led to George's home. It wasn't the prettiest part of Blossom Meadow, but *inside* George's burrow was a different story. Erin poked her head into the entrance, which was lined with yellow and orange flowers. "George, are you there?" she called.

"Puppies, is that you?" a low voice replied. "Oh, do come in!"

The three best friends shuffled inside, one by one. As always, every available space in George's home was filled with bright bunches of flowers. Amber was relieved not to see any bluebells — they'd recently helped make sure the fairies' home in Bluebell Grove was protected by persuading all the creatures in Blossom Meadow not to pick the slow-growing flowers.

The puppies jumped up on to three tree-trunk seats around George's large log dining table. It was piled so high with flower garlands, the puppies could barely see over them.

"They're for tonight. Do you like them?" George asked, clapping his paws together.

"What's happening tonight?" Erin asked at the same time as Amber said, "Yes, they're lovely!"

George beamed. "Why, it's the Blossom Banquet! I thought that was why you were here. You are coming, aren't you?"

"So that's why everyone's so busy," Kayla said, her curly brown tail wagging in relief.

There was nothing wrong after all! "Yes, we'd love to come," she added, "if we're invited?"

George slapped a leathery paw on the dining table, making the garlands bounce. "Of course you are! You're just as much a part of Blossom Meadow as anybody. Now, have you entered the Dandelion Dance yet? There's isn't much time left before the noon deadline!"

Erin's golden ears pricked up. She remembered George mentioning the dance competition the last time they'd been in Blossom Meadow. "Oh yes, we'd love to," she said.

George waved them towards the burrow entrance. "Then as much as I'd love you to stay for elevenses, you'd better go and find Edna Mouse. She lives in the sycamore tree at the very end of Lupin Lane."

The puppies said goodbye to George and quickly left the burrow. They had to hurry – Lupin Lane was all the way past Violet Green and over Buttercup Bridge. They ran as fast as their legs would carry them. Amber wasn't sure she'd ever quite get used to running as a puppy, but it was fun all the same, galloping along and feeling the soft ground beneath each of her four paws. She was on the school athletics team, and wondered if she was faster at running as a puppy than as a girl.

They scampered off the bridge and turned right on to Lupin Lane. Kayla pointed out the sycamore right at the end. She raced out in front, running between the rows of towering purple and pink flowers that grew either side. The puppies soon arrived at the base of the gnarly tree trunk. It was the only tree around, so they knew this had to be the one. They were doubly sure when a little white face peeped out of a hole near the bottom.

"Are you here to register for the Dandelion Dance?" the mouse squeaked. "You're just in time!"

"Yes!" barked Erin. "I'm Erin, and this is Kayla and Amber." She turned to her friends, and realized she hadn't actually asked them if they wanted to dance in the competition. But luckily they were

grinning – they were used to Erin's quick decisions, and they liked to dance just as much as she did.

Edna wrote their names down on the tiniest clipboard they had ever seen. "Wonderful!" she squeaked. "We've never had puppies in the Dandelion Dance before. See you tonight, and good luck!"

"Thank you, Edna," Amber called as they left the sycamore tree. Then she looked at Kayla and Erin. "What are we going to do for the dance?" Deep down Amber felt a bit nervous about dancing in front of everyone. "We haven't danced together for ages!"

"Don't worry," Erin replied. "We have the whole afternoon to practise!"

Kayla nodded, making her fluffy brown ears bounce. "Come on, let's go and find somewhere quiet."

But they didn't get very far. Halfway

along Lupin Lane, they heard tiny voices calling to them. When they turned around, they saw the blue figures of two fairies hovering in the air.

"Bran and Sen!" said Amber as she saw the fairy twins. "Are you all right?"

The fairies' faces were wrinkled with worry. "Not really," Sen replied as they came to land. "We were wondering if you might be able to help…"

Chapter 2

Tasty Treats and Spinning Sprites

"Of course!" barked Erin. "What do you need help with?"

"We don't know where the gnomes are," Bran squeaked. "They're meant to be doing the decorations for the banquet with us. We agreed that they would do all the daisy chains to drape over the tables, and we would do the lights."

"And we don't have time to search the meadow for them," Sen added. "We're too busy arranging the lanterns!"

Kayla stepped forward and gently put a paw on Sen's little blue foot. "Don't worry, we'll find them," she said. "They must be in Blossom Meadow somewhere!"

"Oh, thank you so very much!" Bran fluttered his golden wings and took Sen's hand. "We'd better get back to the lights. Thank you, puppies!"

"Yes, thank you," Sen whispered as they

sped off into the blue sky.

Erin, Amber and Kayla turned to each other. "Where should we start?" Amber wondered. "The meadow is huge!"

"Yes, but we've already been to quite a lot of places today," Kayla pointed out. "We didn't see the gnomes, so we don't need to check those places again."

Erin nodded her golden head in agreement. "Let's start with Poppy Place," she suggested, "and we can work back from there." Poppy Place was at the other side of Blossom Meadow from Bluebell Grove.

Amber was feeling tired from a whole day at Doggy Delight. But that didn't stop her sprinting on all fours towards Poppy Place. The sooner they found the gnomes, the sooner they could put the fairies' minds at rest ... and the sooner they could start practising their dance!

When they arrived at the huge field of bright orange poppies, they spotted a group of dragonflies fluttering about. "We could ask them if they've seen the gnomes," Amber said, nodding at the pretty green, purple and blue insects.

The puppies ran up to the dragonflies, who were hovering just above the ground, staring at some leaves that were scattered about.

"The honey nectar with rose sorbet is the best," a purple dragonfly buzzed, pointing a wing at one of the leaves.

A green dragonfly flew over. "No way!"

it said. "The blueberry mess with chestnut caramel is *much* better!"

Kayla coughed, and the dragonflies turned around to look at the puppies. "Oh good!" said a blue dragonfly. "You can help us choose which dessert we should serve at the banquet tonight!"

The dragonflies scooped up the leaves and brought them towards Erin, Kayla and Amber.

"Oh yum, I wish we could!" Erin said. "But we need to look for the gnomes. I'm sorry! Have you seen them?"

The dragonflies shook their wings. "Sorry, no," the purple one replied. "But please can you help us? It won't take long, I promise. We'll never decide otherwise!"

Kayla looked across at her friends, who all shrugged. "All right then. But we really do need to hurry."

The puppies tasted each leaf in turn. All the desserts were delicious – even the ones that sounded strange, like nettle tart with redcurrant icing, and violet bites with acorn sprinkles.

"Could you serve them all?" Amber suggested, thinking she'd never be able to decide.

"Oh, now that's a top idea!" the green dragonfly said. "Why didn't we think of that? We'll do a selection! Thanks for your help, puppies."

The friends smiled and waved, then scampered away. They were no closer to finding the gnomes, and they hadn't had any time to practise their dance, either.

"How about Primrose Pond next?" Kayla said. They were already running in that direction – away from Poppy Place. The pond was just on the other side of Badger Burrows.

Erin and Amber nodded as they ran, their tails bouncing behind them. It was where the water sprites lived – maybe they'd seen the gnomes. As the puppies arrived through a line of oak trees, they saw the sprites spinning about on the grass beside the pond. "That's weird," barked Erin. "What are the water sprites doing out of the water?"

One of the turquoise sprites stopped

spinning and leapt over to the puppies on her long webbed feet. Her little fins shuddered at her side and her green hair flowed down past her waist. It was their friend, Wilma. "We're practising our gymnastics performance for tonight," she explained. "And you've come just in time! Want to have a sneak peek?"

Amber frowned. They couldn't afford to lose any more time.

"How long is it?" Kayla asked. If it was only short, then it would be fine, she decided.

Wilma smiled. "Oh, just a few minutes!"

Erin clapped her paws together. "Of course we can," she said, and nestled her bottom into the grass.

Her friends sat down beside her. "What about our dance?" Amber whispered. "And the gnomes?"

"This won't take long – Wilma said so," Kayla replied. "We can't really say no. It wouldn't be very nice."

The water sprites began. Rather than being a water performance, which is what the puppies had seen the sprites do before, this was out of the water. But they almost made it look as if they were swimming, as they spun and skipped and swirled around each other.

Well, they did for a few seconds, anyway. And then they'd go wrong – spinning the wrong way and catching the wrong hand and getting confused about which part they were at. And every time they made a mistake, they started again from the beginning, which meant it took a lot longer than a few minutes!

At last, they finished, spinning into a towering sprite pyramid, balancing on each other's shoulders. The puppies clapped. "It was brilliant," said Amber, jumping up so they could continue their search for the gnomes right away.

"I mean, you made a few mistakes," Erin added. "But I just know you'll do it perfectly tonight!"

"Will you watch again?" Wilma asked. "Just to make sure?"

Kayla shook her head, making her little brown ears flap from side to side. "We really have to go, I'm sorry. I don't suppose you've seen the gnomes, have you?" she added. "We need to find them."

"Oh, you'll never find them!" said Wilma. "No one even knows where they live!"

"*I* know," another water sprite squeaked from the still-towering pyramid. "They live underground at Honeysuckle Hill."

"Oh, thank you!" Amber barked, and began running towards the oak trees right away. Erin and Kayla were quickly on her tail. Now all they had to do was get to Honeysuckle Hill and make sure the gnomes were ready with their decorations. Then they could tell the fairies and have enough time left to practise their dance!

Chapter 3

Friendly Foxes and Special Guests

The puppies were back on Honeysuckle Hill, where they'd arrived in Blossom Meadow earlier that day. But it felt as if a lot more time had passed.

"Look, there's a hole," yelled Erin. "That must be it!" She ducked inside before her friends could reply, so they had no choice but to follow her.

They chased Erin's wagging golden tail along a narrow, dark passageway until Erin suddenly stopped. Kayla couldn't slow down in time, and she bumped into Erin … and behind Kayla, Amber did the same, crashing into Kayla's fluffy brown back legs.

"What happened?" Kayla yelped, rubbing her bashed nose with a paw.

Erin turned around, her big brown eyes even larger than normal. "There's someone here," she whispered. "But it's not a gnome!"

Kayla and Amber peeped over Erin's

shoulders ... and saw the brown and white face of a large fox. Amber began backing away out of the passage. Would the fox be angry that they had barged into his home?

"Hey, puppies!" the fox said, beaming. "What's up?"

Amber stopped. The fox didn't sound angry, in fact, he seemed happy to see them!

As if to show it, the fox held up a paw for Erin to give him a high five. "Welcome to our den! I'm Francis. Come and meet the rest of the gang..."

The puppies didn't really have any choice but to follow – after all, they had

just barged into the fox's home. They were lucky he didn't think they were rude!

Kayla sniffed the air as they padded after the fox. She could smell something amazing – and the aroma only got stronger the more they walked. When they arrived in a small cavern, she could see why – it was filled with platters of food. Beetroot crisps and cheese scones and vegetable tarts, if she wasn't mistaken! Kayla's mouth began to water, even after all the desserts they'd eaten with the dragonflies.

Erin looked around at the foxes dotted about the cavern. "We're … um … looking for the gnomes. Are they down here somewhere?"

Francis chuckled. "Gnomes? They don't live here! Reckon it'd be the last place they'd want to live – with us. They're secretive types, those gnomes are."

"But the sprites said this is where we'd find them," Amber whispered to her friends.

"Oh, those sprites were pulling your leg!" Francis continued. "You know how they like jokes. And today is the one day of the week we agreed they could play their pranks..."

The puppies looked at each other. Could it be true? The water sprites didn't know what the puppies were trying to do after all – the one who'd played the prank probably hadn't meant any harm. But

now they'd wasted even more time. Kayla groaned. Normally she had a good sense of humour, but this wasn't very funny.

"While you're here," Francis went on, "I don't suppose you could help us carry out the food we've rustled up for the banquet? It'll save us a few trips."

The puppies couldn't really say no. They grabbed a plate each in their front paws, and walked out of the cavern on their hind legs, following the passageway out into the open air. The meadow looked different compared with when they'd gone in – dusk

was falling, and the sky was a deep plum purple, with a full moon rising just above.

It was all Erin could do not to snaffle one of the cheese scones she was carrying in her paws as they strode towards Violet Green, where the Blossom Banquet was being held. The place had been transformed. There were lanterns everywhere, and lines of wooden tables that were already half-full with food. Flower bunting was strung up on poles, criss-crossing the tables, and colourful silk was draped over each log chair.

As the puppies placed the plates of food on a free table, Amber suddenly gasped. Erin and Kayla looked to see what was wrong, and Erin let out a shocked bark. There in front of them were three majestic unicorns.

"Oh, let me introduce you," George

said. The badger bustled over, his paws full of flower garlands. "Amber, Kayla and Erin, this is Isabelle, Cora and Lei. The unicorns are from Blossom Wood, over the Great Hedge."

The puppies gawped at the unicorns. The tallest one – Cora – had a long flowing yellow mane. The smallest one – Lei – had a shorter pink mane, and the middle one – Isabelle – had a bright red wavy mane. The creatures beamed at Erin, Kayla and Amber.

"It's so nice to meet you," Isabelle neighed.

"We can't wait for the banquet," Lei added, with a shake of her mane. "That's why we're a bit early!"

Cora moved to the side and Amber saw she had a badger on her back! The animal slid down to the ground and held out his

paw. "I'm Bobby," he said in a gravelly voice. "George's cousin!"

George wrapped his paws around Bobby in a hug. "Will you come and help me with the flower garlands?" he asked.

Bobby nodded his stripy head. "I'd be delighted to!" he said, and the cousins lumbered away.

"Oh look, there are the fairies," Kayla said as she saw Bran, Sen and the rest of the fairies fluttering into Violet Green, their wings shimmering in the light from the lanterns.

Amber bounced from paw to paw, worries whirling around her brain. They were going to have to tell them they hadn't had any luck in finding the gnomes yet...

"We haven't found them!" Erin blurted, before the fairies could even ask. "I'm so sorry!"

Bran landed and put his blue-tinged hands to his head. "Oh dear, oh dear. What has happened to the gnomes and their decorations?"

The next moment, Sen landed next to her twin. "We don't care about the decorations so much — we just don't want the gnomes to miss out!"

Chapter 4

The Great Hedge

"Don't worry," Kayla said. "We'll fix it, won't we?" She turned to the golden Labrador and cockapoo beside her and they both nodded furiously. The three puppies scampered away across Violet Green, thinking about where they could look next.

"Thank you!" they heard the fairies calling after them. "You puppies are the best."

Amber tensed up as they ran. They wouldn't be the best if they couldn't find the gnomes. And there would definitely be no time to rehearse their dance now. They wouldn't be able to join in the competition.

They were heading towards Buttercup Bridge. Just as they were about to cross it, their friend Trudge appeared from beneath it. Trudge was one of the trolls who lived under the bridge. He had a large grey head, wide green eyes, big pointy ears and shoulder-length blonde hair. He wasn't wearing his usual brown, patched dungarees today, but a smart black suit, with his long dark-green shoes poking out from the bottom of the trousers.

Erin suddenly panicked that he was going to stop them crossing the bridge – it had happened before, when Trudge had been unhappy. But he only grinned at the puppies

and waved them across. "See you at the party?" he asked as more trolls popped up from below the bridge.

"Of course!" Erin barked in reply as they ran past. "We'll be there soon!"

At the other side of the bridge, the puppies skidded to a stop. "Where should we go?" asked Kayla. "We're close to Bluebell Grove here – surely the fairies would have seen the gnomes if they lived nearby."

Amber was looking around slowly, sniffing the air, which had a faint tinge of smoke from the lanterns in Violet Green. "Not if they want to stay hidden. I know they weren't in the burrows beneath Honeysuckle Hill, but maybe they're somewhere else underground…"

"So should we look for holes?" said Erin, staring at the ground.

"That's a good idea!" Kayla said, swishing her curly tail.

The three best friends angled their heads towards the ground, using the moon's bright white beam as light. *This could take ages*, Amber thought, as they walked in a line, staring downwards.

"What's this?" Erin said suddenly, poking a paw into a little hole in the grass. "Oh no — it's just a dip."

They kept going, their eyes peeled for anything that could be a gnome hole. But they didn't even know how big the gnomes were. Kayla guessed they were small — littler than the puppies at least — but she realized they should have asked the fairies more about what they looked like.

"Ouch!" yelped Amber, jumping backwards as she hit something prickly. She looked up and saw a high, leafy green hedge. She'd been so busy looking downwards she hadn't seen it coming.

Kayla gasped. "The Great Hedge!" They'd never got this close to it before. It towered up, almost as tall as a tree, and stretched from left to right as far as they could see.

Erin turned around, searching the ground away from it. But Amber was still staring up at the hedge, her shiny black head tilted to one side. "If I wanted to hide," she said, "the

back wants is she ill see them finding dirt
looks up and says brightly Erin heed to

Great Hedge would be the perfect place…"

"You're right!" Kayla said, and pushed her
furry brown face into the branches. "There's
loads of space in here."

At her friends' words, Erin spun back
again. "Then we should check it out right
now!" She dived into the hedge, front
paws first. Kayla and Amber shrugged at
each other and followed her in.

"Gnomes?" Erin began to shout.

"Are you—"

"Shh," Kayla said, cutting Erin off. "If they're hiding in here, we don't want to scare them."

Erin's golden cheeks flushed red. "You're right, sorry."

It was almost pitch-black inside the Great Hedge, but the puppies could see quite well in the dark – much better than they could as humans. Thin branches stretched up, up, up all around, but there was room enough for them, as long as they walked carefully. Kayla nudged something on the ground with her little brown nose. "A daisy!" she whispered. "What's that doing in here?"

"The fairies said the gnomes were in charge of the daisy chains for the banquet," Erin remembered.

Amber nodded. "This must be a clue!"

The puppies saw a couple more daisies just

ahead ... and then a couple more.

"It's a trail," panted Kayla. "The gnomes must have dropped the daisies!"

They followed the path of daisies slowly.

"It's like a dot-to-dot," Erin said.

"Oh, I love those!" Kayla had lots of dot-to-dots pinned up on her bedroom wall at home, in between other pictures she'd drawn.

Amber's little black ears pricked up even higher than normal. "I hear something!"

she whispered.

The puppies stopped and listened carefully. "You take them, Hillbean, please." The voice was tiny, but tinkling rather than squeaky – like a triangle being played.

"No, I really can't," someone replied in a similar light voice. "Don't make me..."

"Hello?" Erin called, remembering to do it gently this time.

There was a shuffling sound. "Who's there?"

"We're puppies – and friends of the fairies," Kayla explained. "We know you're shy, but we just want to help." She peeped her fluffy brown ears over a branch so the gnomes could see her – and she could see them. The gnomes were almost exactly how Kayla had imagined them, with pointy red hats, long white hair and tunics tied with black belts.

As Kayla spoke, the gnomes ducked their heads, as if they didn't want anyone to see

them. They huddled together even closer.

"We can take the daisy chains for you," Kayla went on. "If you really don't want to go to the banquet."

One of the gnomes poked her head up. Her long hair was in two plaits, and she wore a bright red tunic. "You'd do that for us?" she said, her voice like the patter of rain.

"Of course," Amber said. She felt sorry for the gnomes. Amber wasn't really shy, but she did worry a lot, and that meant she sometimes got anxious when speaking to people. She could understand how the gnomes felt.

The gnome's eyes filled with tears. "Thank you, dear puppies. That really is kind – and such a relief. We'll go and get the daisy chains for you…"

The gnomes shuffled away, further along the hedge until the puppies couldn't see them any more.

Erin shook her golden head sadly. "It's such a shame the gnomes will miss out on the banquet. It looks as if it's going to be *amazing*."

Chapter 5

Blossom Banquet

By the time the gnomes returned with the daisy chains, Amber had an idea. She shuffled forward a little and barked gently, "I've thought of something."

The gnomes lifted their heads and waited for Amber to continue.

"Everyone's at the banquet already. So what if you came with us, but stayed at the edge of Violet Meadow? We can make sure you're not bothered by anyone. That way you could see the banquet – and your beautiful decorations hung up." She nodded at the daisy chains, which weren't just in single strings but plaited together into stunning long ropes of flowers.

"You could even hide under Buttercup Bridge," added Kayla, pressing her paws together hopefully.

The red-hatted creatures looked at each other … and slowly began to smile. "It's a great idea," said the gnome in the blue tunic. "Thank you."

The puppies lifted the daisy chains over their shoulders, winding them carefully around their necks so they didn't drag on the ground. They walked slowly out of the Great Hedge, taking care not to catch the flower chains on the branches, with the gnomes following behind.

Blossom Meadow was completely silent – there was no rustle of insects in the grass, no twittering of birds. "Everyone's definitely at the banquet," Erin said. "It's so quiet it's almost spooky!"

When they scampered up over Buttercup Bridge, distant chattering and laughing filled their ears. As they got to the top of the bridge, they could see Violet Green filled with every kind of creature.

The gnomes kept behind the puppies, shuffling down the other side of the bridge. When they reached the carpet of buttercups at the base, the gnomes stopped and ducked underneath the wooden slats.

"We'll leave you here then," Kayla said to the gnomes quietly. "I hope you can enjoy the banquet a bit!"

Erin and Amber waved to the gnomes, and they nodded their pointy hats in reply. The puppies scampered quickly across Violet Green – by the sound of the beautiful birdsong coming from the banquet area, it had already begun! When they arrived, what looked like a hundred hummingbirds were hovering over the banquet tables, singing their lilting song.

Kayla, Amber and Erin quickly draped the daisy chains over the tables – around the bowls of food and place settings. Then they found three empty log chairs and sat down, their tails wagging.

Beside Erin, a snowy owl whispered in her ear. "The daisy plaits are gorgeous. It must have taken you ages to make them!"

Erin shook her head, making her golden ears flap about. "Oh no, it wasn't us! It was the gnomes. They're too shy to come to the banquet, but they still made the decorations."

"That was kind of them," the owl replied. "I'm Katie, by the way. And these are my friends Alex and Eva." The beautiful white owl pointed to a little owl opposite her, and a barn owl sitting the other side. They each waved a wing and smiled.

"I'm Erin – and this is Amber and Kayla." The puppies smiled back.

Everyone we meet here is so friendly,

thought Amber. *I wish it was like this back home.*

The barn owl pointed at the flower garlands lying on the table in front of the puppies. "Don't forget to put those on," she whispered.

"George's garlands!" said Kayla. She slipped hers over her furry brown head and grinned, looking around for George. She spotted him at the very end of the same table, sitting between a duck and a frog.

The hummingbirds' song came to an end, and they went back to their seats. George banged a paw on the table and stood up on his chair. "Welcome to the Blossom Banquet," he began. "And an especially warm welcome to those who've joined us from over the Great Hedge in Blossom Wood. It is wonderful to see so many creatures together." His stomach rumbled loudly, and he beamed. "I think that's a sign it's time to start eating. Everyone, dig in!"

Amber didn't know what to try first.

There were mushroom muffins and baked potatoes and fruit skewers laid out in front of her.

"You gotta try-ish," Erin said through a mouthful of pumpkin pie, then swallowed. "It's delicious!"

Amber took a piece and bit into the crumbly pastry. Erin was right – it was the best pie she'd ever tasted, with a rich creamy filling and big chunks of pumpkin.

"You've got a piece of pumpkin stuck on your nose!" Erin told Amber, who

quickly swiped it away with a paw. Although, by the look of all the creatures around them, it didn't matter – many of them were enjoying the feast too much to worry about the food that was stuck to their cheeks, whiskers and wings.

Kayla sighed as she finished off an acorn cup of dandelion juice and wondered which dessert to pick. "I wish the gnomes didn't have to miss out on this!"

"I'm totally stuffed," Erin said, rubbing her full tummy. "But the lemon pudding was too good not to have a second helping!"

After dinner, the water sprites gathered in a circle around the banquet tables to perform their gymnastic display. They must have practised a lot since the puppies saw them earlier, because it was *perfect*. They spun all around, weaving in and out of the tables, flipping forwards and backwards and lifting each other up. They even had ribbons in their hair, which fluttered as they moved, making the display even prettier. The water sprites finished, balancing in a pyramid just like the puppies had seen, and everyone clapped their hands, paws and wings.

George stood up on his chair again and waited for the applause to die down. "And now it's time for the Dandelion Dance competition. Edna Mouse, over to you!"

Edna came rushing forward, followed by three other mice. *They must be the judges!* thought Erin. They lined up at the far side of the dance floor, which was made up of thousands of shiny, flat pebbles placed together like a mosaic. A swarm of fireflies flew over to hover above the area, and suddenly the dance floor was alight. Above them fluttered the hummingbirds who'd sung earlier, and Amber wondered if they'd sing for each of the dances.

Edna held up something tiny and golden. "Hello, everyone! This is the golden dandelion, which will be awarded to the winners of the competition." She might have been a little mouse, but her squeaky voice carried across Violet

Green so everybody could hear it. "First to perform their dance are the Willow Lake Wanderers!"

A group of frogs and toads leapt up and hopped towards the dance floor. They positioned themselves in a line, and began their dance – kicking their legs left and right, waving their arms and nodding their heads. It wasn't the sort of dance that Erin had expected from them at all, but it was still pretty good. The hummingbirds sang a song that perfectly matched the Willow Lake Wanderers' moves, with lots of toots and trumpeting sounds.

Next came the foxes. "We're going to do the foxtrot," one of them said before they began, and everyone laughed.

Then a trio of ducks breakdanced, a group of moles performed a samba, and a clan of badgers did a tap dance – George and Bobby included!

Edna looked at her list. "We have one final dance," she announced. "The puppies!"

Kayla gulped and looked over at her friends. They hadn't practised at all!

Chapter 6

Let's Dance

"We'll have to pull out!" said Amber, bouncing from paw to paw with worry.

Kayla shook her head. "We can't do that. Everyone's looking at us…"

Erin's eyes lit up suddenly. "What about that dance we did at the school fete?"

Amber kept on bouncing. "But I hardly remember it," she said.

"I do!" Erin grinned. "Just follow me, and we'll be fine."

Kayla patted a paw on Erin's golden back. "Good idea! I'm sure it'll come back to us when we start."

And so the three puppies scampered over to the dance floor. The bright lights of the fireflies above meant they could hardly see any of the creatures watching. Amber decided that was a good thing.

Erin looked up at the hummingbirds. "Can you sing something classical?" she asked. They began tweeting a slow and gentle song, and Erin turned to Kayla and Amber. "One, two, three, four..."

They began the simple ballet dance they'd performed over a year ago at school. Amazingly, Erin remembered every single move, and Kayla and Amber tried to copy her as well as they could.

But it wasn't easy — especially now they were puppies and not girls. Amber tripped over her front paws more than once, and Kayla's floppy ears kept getting in her way.

Still, they made it to the end of the dance, ending in an arabesque, where they stood on their front legs with their hind legs lifted high in the air. The audience clapped and cheered. Kayla looked over at Edna and her team of judges, who were

making notes on little pieces of bark. She was sure they wouldn't win, but it had been fun anyway!

They left the dance floor and the judges chatted for a few minutes before Edna called out, "We are ready to announce the winner." She stood in the middle of the dance floor on her tiny white mouse legs. "The golden dandelion goes to the Duck Dance Trio! We had never seen ducks breakdance before, and it really was spectacular. Congratulations."

The three ducks jumped up from their seats and quacked with excitement all the way to the stage. Edna presented them with the golden dandelion and every creature watching whooped as the ducks held their trophy aloft.

"And now I think it's time for everyone to take to the dance floor," Edna added in a squeak. "There's plenty of space for us all!"

The hummingbirds began a jazzy tune, and all the animals, birds, insects and magical creatures rushed to the stage, as if they'd been waiting for this all along. As the puppies danced, the fairies joined them in the air above, swinging each other around as they flew.

Kayla spun around on one paw, and something caught her eye. Was that...? Yes, there in the distance, she could see the gnomes dancing under the bridge.

"I'll be right back," she whispered to Erin and Amber. Kayla ran over to the tables and scooped up some of the leftover food into her paws. Making sure no one saw her, she tiptoed over to Buttercup Bridge on her back paws. "Gnomes, it's only me," she called out quietly when she was near. "I've brought you some food, in case you're hungry."

The gnomes clapped their hands together with glee. "We're starving," the gnome with the plaits replied. "Thank you!"

"You're very welcome!" Kayla tipped the food into the gnomes' hands and nodded. "I'm so glad you're enjoying the banquet too."

The gnomes beamed. "So are we!"

Kayla scampered back to the banquet and joined her friends on the dance floor.

"Is everything OK?" Amber asked.

"Oh yes," Kayla replied. "Everything is perfect. The gnomes are happy. Everyone in Blossom Meadow is happy!"

Erin wasn't sure how long they'd been dancing for, but her paws were beginning to ache. She didn't want the party to end, but she could see all the creatures were starting to get tired. And then the hummingbirds stopped singing and the fireflies fluttered away.

Their friend Chloe flew over. "Puppies, I haven't see you all evening. And now

the banquet is finishing! Your dance was great, by the way."

Kayla laughed. "I'm not sure about that, but I'm glad you liked it!"

Amber grinned at the purple-tipped butterfly. "It's sad that it's the end of the evening, but I'm actually really tired." It wasn't surprising — they'd had a whole day back in their world before their day in Blossom Meadow.

Erin and Kayla nodded.

"But hopefully we'll be back soon!" said Erin.

The puppies said goodbye to their friends in Blossom Meadow — old ones like George and new ones like the unicorns. Then it really was time to get home.

They ran towards Blossom Brook, where they wouldn't be seen, and Kayla slipped the collar off her neck from under the flower garland. The three best friends held on to the collar tightly, and right away felt tingles zipping up from their paws. Purple sparks began to shoot around them — different to the white ones that had brought them to the meadow. Soon they were surrounded by a purple cloud, and they could no longer feel the ground beneath their paws as they were lifted up...

The tingles from the collar died down, and Amber realized she could feel the ground under her paws again — though of course, she didn't have paws any more, but feet! She looked around at Erin and Kayla as the purple gleam disappeared and all they could see was the inside of the storeroom at Doggy Delight.

"Girls!" came a shout.

"My dad!" said Kayla. The next second, he opened the storeroom door. The best friends tried to look normal – as if they hadn't just been on an amazing adventure in Blossom Meadow, but were just returning the grooming things to their shelf.

Kayla's dad frowned. "Oh, you three look exhausted. It's time to go home anyway." His frown deepened. "Where did you get those garlands from?"

The girls looked down and saw the flower garlands still dangling around their necks.

"Um … we've had them on all day!" Erin fibbed quickly, crossing her fingers behind her back.

Kayla's dad shook his head in confusion. "Have you? I must not have noticed. To tell you the truth, I'm tired too. Let's get home, order a takeaway and watch a film. Erin and Amber, I'll call your parents to let them know. You definitely deserve it after all your hard work here. Which film would you like to watch?"

"*Bolt*!"

"*Lady and the Tramp*!"

"*Beethoven*!"

Erin, Amber and Kayla said at exactly the same time.

Kayla's dad laughed. "You three love dogs more than anything, don't you?" he said.

The best friends grinned at each other.

They couldn't argue with that. They'd had a day surrounded by dogs at Doggy Delight – followed by a day being *actual dogs* in Blossom Meadow. They'd helped the gnomes and even met some unicorns. They were so tired they weren't sure they'd be able to keep their eyes open to watch a film, but it'd been worth it for their best adventure yet!

Word Search

Can you find the words related to the
banquet in this word search?

G	N	O	M	E	S	A	W	B	V
A	N	B	A	T	M	R	G	U	L
V	R	U	I	D	Y	U	A	G	L
D	E	B	T	A	K	B	R	H	A
C	S	S	N	I	J	L	L	K	N
R	P	C	O	S	M	F	A	J	T
N	Y	Q	P	Y	F	O	N	I	E
E	D	W	B	L	E	D	D	V	R
S	A	R	A	H	G	C	S	H	N
F	S	P	R	I	N	K	L	E	S

 GARLANDS   LANTERNS   SPRINKLES

 DAISY   GNOMES

You can find the answers at the back of the book.

George Fact File

Want to get to know George the badger better? Here are some fun facts about him…

Name: George Badger

Age: He'd rather not say

Family: Has a cousin called Bobby who lives in Blossom Wood

Favourite dog: He could never choose between Kayla, Erin and Amber!

Favourite hobby: Baking

Favourite book: *The Wind in the Willows* by Kenneth Grahame

Likes: Taking naps

Dislikes: Unfairness

Where are the Gnomes?

Can you spot four gnomes that are
hiding among the party guests?

You can find the answers at the back of the book.

Did You Know?

 Bees beat their wings 200 times a second!

 Foxes can run up to 30 miles an hour.

 Hedgehogs have over 5000 spikes on their back.

 A mouse can swim and tread water for up to three days!

 Some sunflowers can grow up to 3 metres tall, that's as tall as 6 Labrador puppies stacked on top of one another!

Blossom Banquet

You have been invited to the Blossom
Banquet! Can you decorate the invitation?
You could use the flowers and lovely food
that was eaten in the story as inspiration.

To:_____

You are cordially invited to the Blossom
Banquet at Violet Green.
From: The animals of Blossom Meadow

Dot-to-dot Daisy

Kayla loves dot-to-dots! Follow the path of
the dots to reveal the daisy!

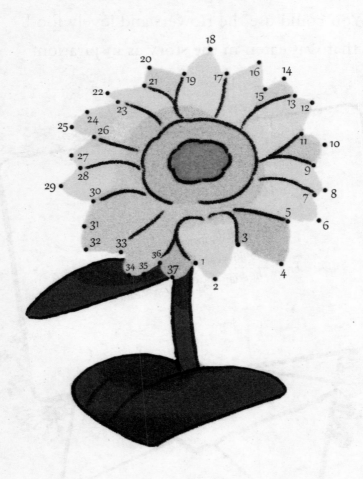

Meet

The Owls of Blossom Wood

in these magical books

The Owls of Blossom Wood
A Magical Beginning
Catherine Coe

The Owls of Blossom Wood
To the Rescue
Catherine Coe

The Owls of Blossom Wood
Lost and Found
Catherine Coe

The Owls of Blossom Wood
The Birthday Party
Catherine Coe

The Owls of Blossom Wood
Save the Day
Catherine Coe

The Owls of Blossom Wood
An Enchanted Wedding
Catherine Coe

Meet

The Unicorns of Blossom Wood

in these magical books

Meet

The Puppies of Blossom Meadow

in these magical books

Catherine Coe

Super cute puppy games
and quizzes inside!

BLOSS

The
Puppies of
Blossom
Meadow

Fairy Friends

Catherine Coe

Super cute puppy game and jigsaw inside!

The Puppies of Blossom Meadow

Mischief and Magic

Read on for a sneak peek of
the third book in the series!

Catherine Coe

Super cute puppy games
and quizzes inside!

The
Puppies of
Blossom
Meadow

Sprite Surprise

Chapter 1

Hot, Hot, Hot

Hot sunshine shone down on Amber, Kayla and Erin as they followed Kayla's dad into Doggy Delight, the dog kennels where he worked. The three best friends were helping out during the school holidays.

Inside the door of the red-brick Victorian house, Erin wiped away the blonde bits of hair that had stuck to her forehead. "It's so hot today!" she said.

As Amber and Kayla nodded, a German shepherd in the hallway woofed.

"It looks as if Poppy agrees," Kayla said, patting her favourite dog on the head. Poppy's pink tongue was waggling even more than usual today.

Kayla's dad pinched the end of his nose. "Phew – I think it might be a good idea to give the dogs baths this morning! And as it's so warm, we can do it in the garden. Amber, Erin, Kayla, would you be able to go to the storeroom and find the doggy paddling p—"

"Yes!" the girls shouted before Kayla's dad had finished, and ran through the house and into the garden. They had a secret inside the storeroom, and they couldn't wait to get there.

"Hi, Matt, hi, Spot, hi, Rosie, hi, Jeff," Erin called to the dogs they passed. She had a brilliant memory, and already knew the name of every single one of the dogs staying at the kennels by heart.

Each of the dogs — a sausage dog, a French bulldog, a chihuahua and a greyhound — barked gently back, and the three friends grinned. They loved

being here, no matter how much work it sometimes was. They couldn't have pets at home because it wasn't allowed in their block of flats, so this was the next best thing!

They reached the shed at the end of the garden and entered the storeroom. Kayla and Erin ran straight towards a cupboard on the far wall, but Amber hung back.

"Shouldn't we get the doggy paddling pools out before we go to Blossom Meadow?" she said, pulling nervously on her long brown hair.

Erin frowned. "Don't be silly!" she yelled. "Now's our chance to use the magic collar!" She jumped up to find it on the top of the cupboard ... but she was shorter than her friends, and couldn't reach.

"I don't think Erin meant to shout at

you – did you, Erin?" Kayla nudged her. "We would just really, *really* like to use the collar now…"

"Sorry, Amber," said Erin, her cheeks going red. "You weren't being silly and I shouldn't have shouted. It's just that no time passes when we're in Blossom Meadow, remember? So when we get back we'll be able to fetch the paddling pools, and Kayla's dad won't know the difference!"

Amber's brown eyes widened. "Of course. I was worrying over nothing, just like my mum always says I do!" She jumped up and down, pointing to the cupboard. "Quick, get the collar then…"

Kayla leapt up to grab it, her black topknots bouncing around. She brought it down and the girls stared at the purple collar in Kayla's hands, which sparkled brightly in the sunshine streaming through the storeroom window. The shiny silver name tag swung on its chain like a pendulum clock, and the word Blossom blurred as it moved back and forth.

Erin and Amber reached out so that all three girls were holding the collar. Then they held their breath...

The next moment, white sparkles began spinning off the collar, whizzing around them like a hurricane. "Don't let go!" Erin squealed, as her feet lifted off the floor. The three friends rose higher and higher, and the storeroom disappeared in the cloud of sparkles.

Amber closed her eyes, just as she always did. It felt somehow safer that way! Her skin tingled with magic, like she'd been covered in popping candy, and her ears seemed to crackle with electricity.

Magic rushed around them, zipping and glittering, raising them ever higher... But soon Kayla felt solid ground beneath her legs again. "You can open your eyes now," she said to Amber softly.

"We're back, we're back!" shouted Erin. She spun around and stared down at her furry golden legs and paws — for

every time the friends arrived in Blossom Meadow, they were no longer girls, but puppies!

Erin finally stopped spinning to look at Kayla and Amber, who were now a fluffy brown cockapoo and a sleek black terrier. Erin was a cute golden Labrador, with big floppy ears and a very waggly tail. They were standing by the emerald-green water of Primrose Pond, which was encircled with pretty little flowers in yellow, red, pink, purple and orange.

Kayla scooped her head down to put on the Blossom collar for safekeeping, and felt wet all of a sudden. "Oh no, it's raining!" she said, shaking out her fur.

Kayla shook herself too, then looked up at the sky. "But there aren't any clouds – it's just as hot here as it is at home."

A frown crossed Erin's golden forehead. "So where is the rain coming from?"

"I don't know," Amber replied. "But let's get under that tree before we get soaked!"

They scampered to the nearest tree – a tall, wide oak with giant bright-green

leaves. Kayla tilted her head and listened.
"That's weird. It isn't raining here. I can't
hear any raindrops on the leaves at all."

Amber pointed a black paw across to
Primrose Pond. "It's only raining over there,
look!"

Sure enough, they could see water was
only falling at the edge of the pond. It
glistened in the sunshine as it spattered
down on to the primroses.

Erin leapt up and beckoned to her friends.
"Come on – let's go over there and find out
what's going on!

Answer Sheet:

G	N	O	M	E	S	A	W	B	V
A	N	B	A	T	M	R	G	U	L
V	R	U	I	D	Y	U	A	G	L
D	E	B	T	A	K	B	R	H	A
C	S	S	N	I	J	L	L	K	N
R	P	C	O	S	M	F	A	J	T
N	Y	Q	P	Y	F	O	N	I	E
E	D	W	B	L	E	D	D	V	R
S	A	R	A	H	G	C	S	H	N
F	S	P	R	I	N	K	L	E	S

Would you like more animal puzzles and activities?

Want sneak peeks of other books in the series, including the Owls and Unicorns of Blossom Wood?

Fancy flying across the treetops in the magical Blossom Wood game?

Then check out the Blossom Wood and Blossom Meadow website at:

blossomwoodbooks.com